Juniper Kai:
Super Spy

Laura Gehl • illustrated by Alexandria Neonakis

two lions

For my spy-tacular daughter, Tessa,
who is even more curious, creative,
intelligent, resourceful, and lovable
than Juniper Kai
—L. G.

To my younger sisters, Ereni and Gina,
and my little brother, George
—A. N.

Published by Two Lions, New York

www.apub.com

Amazon, the Amazon logo, and Two Lions are trademarks of Amazon.com, Inc., or its affiliates.

ISBN-13: 9781542043328 (hardcover)
ISBN-10: 1542043328 (hardcover)

The illustrations are rendered in digital media.

Book design by Tanya Ross-Hughes
Printed in China

First Edition

10 9 8 7 6 5 4 3 2 1

Juniper Kai was born to be a spy. She could crack ten codes before breakfast and find twenty-five clues before lunch.

Her dresser drawers were stuffed with Spy-o-Scopes, fingerprint powder, and a spectacular collection of wigs.

But as the only kid on her street,
Juniper never had anybody to play with.
I Spy didn't work with one person.
Neither did spy-and-go-seek.
Juniper wished super spy
James Bond lived nearby.

Mom and Dad used to play with Juniper.
Dad had lots of good fort-building ideas.

And Mom never minded when Juniper
beat her at Crazy Eights.

But over the last couple of weeks, something had changed.
Suddenly, Dad was too busy to play. Mom was too tired.

And Mom and Dad kept whispering to each other. Juniper felt a bit left out.

"Fine!" Juniper announced to herself. It didn't matter if she had nobody to play with. Because Juniper Kai was born to be a spy. And spies work alone.

Before bed, Juniper organized her disguises, alphabetized her code-breaking manuals, and charged up her genuine James Bond spy camera. Juniper was ready for her newest mission: to find out *exactly* what was going on with Mom and Dad.

The next day, Juniper got to work.
Donning her favorite mustache and her
Super-Ear listening device, Juniper caught
a few words of Mom's phone call with Grandma.

"So exciting"

"Lots of work"

"Huge change"

But Mom was playing Mozart in the background,
so Juniper couldn't hear the rest.

With her best Spy-o-Scope,
Juniper observed Dad in the guest room.

He seemed to be building something. It looked more like a jail than a fort.
But why would Dad need a jail?

Two days later, Juniper found a note written in Mom's handwriting. It was obviously in code.

But even with her code-breaker wheel and five different code-breaking manuals, Juniper couldn't decrypt the message.

On Saturday, Juniper spied Dad reading in his study.
She attached her spy camera to a remote-control helicopter
and maneuvered the chopper to peek at his book.

That didn't help either.

Juniper's spy mission was a complete failure!
Defeated, she flopped into bed with her
top-secret triple-locking
spy notebook.

Suddenly, Juniper's perimeter alarm started flashing.
Grabbing her night-vision goggles, Juniper looked outside.

Dad was putting large boxes in the garden shed. She had to investigate!

Juniper waited until Mom and Dad went to sleep.
She didn't need a Super-Ear listening device
to hear Dad's snores.

Pulling on her trench coat and super-silent spy shoes, Juniper crept outside.

She took her lock pick set out of her pocket and unlocked the shed.
She slowly opened the door, turned on her Spy-De-LIGHT, and . . .

. . . a different kind of light flashed on in Juniper's brain.

The most important mission
of Juniper's life was about to begin!

The next day at breakfast, Juniper said, "I think we should name the baby James. James is a good name for a spy."

"Did you tell her?" Mom and Dad asked each other.

Juniper Kai was born to be a spy.

And spies work alone.

Sometimes.

But **sometimes** a spy needs a good co-agent.
And Juniper Kai knew she was born to be . . .

. . . a **spy-tacular** big sister.